SHARI
and the Greedy Bear

Mizin Publishing LLC, 364 E. Main Street #502, Middletown, Delaware 19709

ISBN: 978-1-7348722-2-4   eISBN: 978-1-7348722-3-1

There once was a bear who lived deep in a forest. His name was Vox and he loved his forest home. He loved his warm cave.

But there was a thing he loved more than anything else in the world, and that was honey. He ate honey morning, noon, and night. The sticky honey covered his mouth and his furry paws. Vox could not get enough of the sweet treat, and he was always looking for more!

One summer day, Vox went for a walk and spotted a big honey hive in a low branch of a tree.

"Honey!" Vox shouted. **"I am the luckiest bear in the whole world for I have found HONEY, and honey is the thing I love most!"**

Vox reached up, up, up, and grabbed the sticky honey hive with both paws.

As he walked on, Vox spotted a honey hive in another tree. This honey hive was even bigger than the first! Vox thought about all the yummy, sticky honey inside this very big hive. But there was a problem. This VERY BIG hive was VERY HIGH up in the branches of the tree. Vox knew that he could not simply reach up and grab it.

"But I must have this honey, too!" said Vox.

Sitting in a nearby tree was Sharp Eye, the eagle. Sharp Eye did not like what he saw and heard. He saw a bear holding a hive in one hand, yet wanting another hive of honey! He heard a bear who wanted more and that he MUST have the honey high in the tree!

No—the eagle did not like what he was seeing and hearing, at all. He knew that this would bring nothing but trouble. Sharp Eye flew down from his tree to be nearer the bear.

"I see that you're carrying a hive filled with honey, Vox. Don't you think that is enough?" Sharp Eye asked him.

Vox looked at the honey hive he was carrying and then he looked up at the hive in the tree. "Yes, I have this honey in my hand," he replied. **"But I want that honey, too!"**

"Vox, you already have a hive filled with lots of honey," the smart eagle said. "You have enough honey. Yet now you want even more honey. You are becoming greedy, Vox. Greed is never good."

But Vox did not listen to Sharp Eye.
He was too busy thinking about all the
honey in the big hive hanging high up
in the tree.

"I am going to get that honey!"
he said.

Vox stretched his paws up as high as he could reach, but it was not enough to get the hive.

"I guess I'll have to climb the tree!" he said. **"But I WILL get that honey!"**

Vox began climbing the tree. When he reached a high branch where the hive was hanging, he pushed himself along until he could almost reach the big hive.

"Careful, Vox," Sharp Eye warned. "I think you may be too heavy for that branch."

Vox didn't want to listen. He pushed himself out to the tip of the branch and reached out a paw to grab the big honey hive.

"If I take just one more step," said Vox. "I will grab the honey."

Just as Vox put his paw
on the hive—

CRACK!

The tree branch broke!

Vox tumbled

down,

down,

down,

from the tree.

And with him came both honey hives.

The sweet, sticky honey spilled from both hives and puddled all around Vox.

"Oh, Vox," Sharp Eye said, "I'm afraid that your greed has caused you to lose everything! You once had a full hive of honey. Now you have none."

Vox sat up and rubbed his sore head. He thought about Sharp Eye's wise words.

"You are right, Sharp Eye," said the bear. "I should have been happy with the honey I had. But I wanted even more. Now I've lost both hives."

Sharp Eye knew that Vox had learned an important lesson.

"We all make mistakes," Sharp Eye told him. "But if we learn from our mistakes, then we don't repeat them."

Vox waved as Sharp Eye flew high into the sky. "Thank you, Sharp Eye!" Vox called. "I won't be greedy again!"

What Do You Think?

- Was Vox happy when he found the first honey hive?

- Did Vox have enough honey when he got the first hive?

- Was Vox greedy for wanting the second hive?

- Did Vox end up losing both hives?

Made in the USA
Middletown, DE
12 July 2021